Philip and the Pooka

AND OTHER IRISH FAIRY TALES

Philip
and the Pooka

AND OTHER IRISH FAIRY TALES

Kathleen Green

Illustrations by Victoria de Larrea

398.21
G

Blairsville Junior High School
Blairsville, Pennsylvania

J. B. LIPPINCOTT COMPANY
New York · Philadelphia

Copyright © 1966 by Kathleen Green
Library of Congress Catalog Card Number 66-10897
Printed in the United States of America
Design by Ruth Smerechniak

SECOND PRINTING

Contents

Philip and the Pooka

AND OTHER IRISH FAIRY TALES

I

Philip and the Pooka

IF PHILIP THE HORSE BREEDER HAD NOT CAUGHT HOLD OF
the Pooka's tail there would have been no story to tell. But
as Philip not only caught hold of it, but gave it a good tug as
well, there is quite a lot to be told.

Philip bred all sorts of horses, and people used to come
from miles around to buy from him. If you wanted a couple
of strong plough horses, or a nice light hunter, you could be
sure to find them in Philip's big pasture. Even the piebald
pony that Tony the Tinker used had been one of Philip's
rearing.

Well, late one evening, Philip went out to the pasture to
look at his horses, and a most extraordinary sight met his
eyes. A little wild, white horse, with a long mane and tail,
was galloping round and round the pasture, with all the

horses, young and old, galloping after him. Even Fanny, the old lame mare, was doing her best to keep up with the others. But, well—as poor Fanny always fell further and further behind the others, the funny part of it was that when she was completely left behind, the whole procession would catch up on her heels again, so that sometimes she was actually leading it!

"Hoy, woah!" shouted Philip, after he had watched for some time. But the horses paid no attention to him.

"That's a wild horse from the hills," said Philip to himself. "And, boys-a-boys, what a beauty! If I could tame him, and train him, he'd be well worth the trouble, so he would."

Of course, Philip should have suspected that the wild white horse was none other than the Pooka, the fairy horse. But he was so busy thinking of some way to catch the strange animal that he never thought, even for a moment, that he was going to do a very foolish thing.

He tried whistling to the horses, and he tried to tempt them with some of the sugar that he always carried in his pockets, but they just went round and round the field and paid no attention. So Philip made a noose in a rope that he had with him, and stood in the field so that the animals had to gallop quite close to him. If only he could throw the noose over the white horse's head!

Round they came, led by the white horse—but instead of going past him they came charging right at him. And instead of throwing his rope Philip had to spring to one side—and as he sprang he made a grab at the white horse and caught hold of the long flying tail.

"Come back here, you," shouted Philip, and then tugged with all his might.

The Pooka was furious. Such an insult! He jumped into

the air off all four legs at once, and then something even worse happened to him. A great handful of his long white tail pulled out, and when he galloped snorting away only about half of his tail was streaming behind him. The other half was in Philip's hand as he went gloomily home, furious that the beautiful horse had escaped him.

Now when Philip went into the kitchen his wife, Maureen, was baking bread, and his wife's mother, who was crippled with rheumatism, was sitting in her wheelchair near the fire.

"What's that you've got in your hand?" she asked curiously.

"Nothing of importance," snapped Philip, in a very bad temper, and threw the tail down on the table.

"It's the horsehair for mending your cushion, mother," said Maureen. "I meant to ask Philip to get me some clippings, and here he's thought of it himself! It's beautiful soft hair, too. Just wait until I get this bread in the oven and I'll stuff your cushion, and make it nice and firm for you again."

"Aye, that'll be fine," wheezed the old woman. "It's great to have a bit of support at your back when you have to sit still all day, indeed it is!"

So Maureen put her bread in to cook, and then she doubled the Pooka's tail over and over and stuffed it into a split in the old woman's cushion. Then she stitched the split together, plumped up the cushion, and tucked it down behind her mother's back.

"Aye, that's comfort," sighed the old woman. But a few minutes later she turned to Philip. "Will you leave me alone," she said, "and don't go pushing into the chair like that."

"I wasn't near you, Mother," protested Philip sulkily.

"You were so," said the old woman. "You gave the chair a great bump. I felt it."

Philip hadn't touched the chair, but three times that evening the old woman complained that something had pushed her, and, indeed, on the third occasion, the chair actually moved across the floor towards the door.

"It's the slope in the floor," said Philip. "And you're that restless tonight I don't know what's up with you." And Philip opened the door and swung it gently to and fro. "Maybe a breath of fresh air will settle you down."

Well—she got fresh air all right! The open door was the very opportunity for which the Pooka's tail had been waiting! You see, it didn't like to be stitched up in a cushion. It wanted to get back to the Pooka, and if it had to bring an old woman and a wheelchair along—well, what of that?

Before Philip or Maureen could do anything about it, the chair had moved quickly out through the open door, down the path and away along the road! They ran after it, of course, but it was soon out of sight.

When Philip told Maureen of the wild white horse she screamed aloud. "Oh," she wailed. "That was the Pooka. We're bewitched! The horsehair has put a spell on the chair, and it's carried Mother off to Tir na nOg. You'll have to go after her."

"Not to Tir na nOg," said Philip firmly. "Certainly not! But I'll get a horse and follow the tracks of the chair as soon as it's daylight."

Well, the only trouble about that was that there wasn't a horse in the pasture, they had all followed the Pooka. However, as soon as the day broke Maureen got out her bicycle and ordered Philip to mount.

"You've lost my mother," she said, "and you'll not come back into this house until you've found her."

So Philip the Horse Breeder mounted his wife's bicycle and went off to search for his mother-in-law and her chair.

It wasn't hard to follow the way she had gone, because everybody he met was talking about the old woman who had passed in the wheelchair.

"It must have had a silent engine hidden in it somewhere," said the man at the garage, where Philip stopped to get his tire pumped. "Never saw anything like it! Just whizzed past, and the old lady waved to me and shouted."

Then Philip overtook Tony the Tinker in the pony cart.

"Your wife's mother is early on the road," he shouted to Philip. "And do you know—my pony shied and then tried to run after that motor-chair, or whatever it is she's driving."

Philip knew that the pony had been trying to follow the Pooka's tail, but he didn't tell the tinker that, just groaned and bent low over his handlebars as he pedaled on. The trouble was that he wasn't even gaining on the old woman; in fact, he was getting left behind.

"Oh, she passed very, very early this morning," said the keeper of the public house, where he stopped about noon to get a sandwich and a glass of beer. "'She must be halfway round Ireland by now, to judge by the speed she was going. She shouted something about a cup of tea, but sure what could I do about that? She was round the bend before you could wink."

Poor Philip groaned again, mounted his bicycle and pedaled off.

"I've heard that a man will follow his wife wherever she goes—but I never heard of a man following his mother-in-law," said the publican, and he laughed until he cried.

All that day Philip pedaled the bicycle, until he was stiff and sore all over. But by late evening he had only reached the part of the country where his mother-in-law had waved to the children at the school break that morning.

"At this rate I'll be pedaling for a month," wailed poor Philip.

But the end of the adventure was much nearer than he thought. Well, it was the same story as when the horses had galloped round, and the old lame mare had got so far behind that she was leading the gallop. Suddenly, out of the gathering dusk, the Pooka whizzed past Philip, coming from *behind* him. The Pooka had been all around Ireland and was starting on the second lap.

But when the Pooka saw poor Philip on the bicycle he slowed down and stopped. Perhaps he thought the joke had gone far enough, or perhaps he was tired of being followed by Philip's horses, Philip's mother-in-law, and the horse breeder himself on the bicycle. Anyway, the white horse stood snorting and pawing the ground, and all Philip's horses came dashing up and began to gambol around the Pooka. Only old Fanny hadn't got there yet—and as it happened she finished her tour of Ireland and arrived home a week later!

Well, Philip had realized by now what was happening, and when the wheelchair came dashing along, hard on the heels of the horses, he dropped his bicycle, caught the chair by the handle, and forced it to stop.

"The cushion!" he shouted. "Give me the cushion, Mother!"

He seized the horsehair cushion from behind her, tore at it until the seams split, and scattered all the hair out. The Pooka's tail flew happily through the air to the Pooka where, being magic, it was able to join itself on. The rest of the hair simply blew away.

"Well, that's what I call a very stupid thing to do,"

snapped the old woman. "This chair is as hard as a board, and my poor old bones will be broken before you have me wheeled home. Destroying my cushion, indeed!"

"Well, I've saved you, haven't I?" cried Philip.

"Saved me?" snorted the old woman. "Saved me, huh! And me having the time of my life! I've never seen so much in one day, never!"

Well, the Pooka must have told Philip's horses to trot off home, for away they went, snorting and tossing their manes, and the Pooka himself bounded off in the opposite direction. And there was poor Philip, with his mother-in-law, her chair, and Maureen's bicycle—and they were almost a hundred miles from home!

It took him a week to get them all safely home, and one would have thought that that would have been the end of it. But it is never safe to pull the Pooka's tail, for who knows when something that is once started is going to end.

Philip thought that he would have had some peace after his adventure, but he had reckoned without his mother-in-law. She had developed a taste for traveling in her chair, and if there wasn't a bit of magic to push it for her—Philip would just have to push it himself. She mended her cushion, bought a new shawl, and from that day forth Philip the Horse Breeder had to spend *all* his free time pushing her around the neighborhood.

2

Big William and the Lop-Eared Creature

Up in the Sperrin Mountains lived the little dark Mountainy Man and his little dark wife, and their flock of small, black-faced sheep.

Now the Mountainy Woman was contented enough to be small herself, but when her baby son, William, was born, she found that she wanted, above anything else, that the baby should grow into a fine tall man. She fed him with everything that she thought might make him grow, but he remained the smallest baby she had ever seen. In the end, she set off one day and tramped up into the heart of the mountain range, to consult the wise old woman who lived there, all alone, in a stone hut.

The old woman was alone, weaving the fine tweed that she sold in order to make a living. She greeted the Mountainy Woman politely and gave her a mug of rabbit broth, and the Mountainy Woman explained about the baby.

"If you could give me some of your herbs, or a tonic to make him grow," she pleaded. "I've always wanted a son like a fine tall policeman. I'll only be contented if he's so big that they call him Big William."

"Fair enough," said the old woman. "Nothing easier. Take this little bottle, good neighbor, and give the child two drops in a glass of milk once a week for the next twenty weeks. After that he'll keep on growing by himself. But mind well, only two drops!"

The Mountainy Woman agreed, gave the old woman some fresh eggs, and went off home with the bottle of tonic. But no sooner was she there than she gave the baby not two, but six drops in a glass of milk. And she kept that up for the twenty weeks.

"He'll be my pride, my Big William," she said to herself.

Well, the name suited him splendidly. By the time he could walk his mother couldn't lift him. When he was five years old the Mountainy Man walked down with him into Tobermore to start him off in school.

"You'd no right to keep the child away from school for so long!" said the Master furiously. "Don't you know there's a law about school attendance;"

"He's only just five, but he's a fine lad," protested the Mountainy Man.

"Five!" snapped the Master. "He's ten if he's a day. He'll have to work hard to catch up with the class. Five, indeed!"

Well, poor Big William hadn't a very happy time in school. In the first place, he couldn't play with the children of his own age. They cried and ran away from him, and when he ran after them they cried more loudly. They couldn't understand that he wanted to be friends.

So Big William kept by himself and did his lessons during the play hour. In this way he got on so fast that he moved from grade to grade, and had finished school by the time he was nine. It was just as well, as he was taller than the Master himself, and he was still growing.

By the time the boy was sixteen the Mountainy Woman was in a panic, and off she went into the mountains again to visit the old woman. Now the old woman and one of the odd little Lop-eared Creatures—the fairy folk of the Sperrins—were enjoying a pot of strong tea in the stone hut. But the Lop-eared Creature warned her that the Mountainy Woman was coming, and she met her visitor outside.

"Well, ma'am, did your boy grow tall enough?"

"Tall enough!" cried the Mountainy Woman. "I can't keep him fed and clothed, he's so big. He's seven foot tall, at sixteen years, and his father's had to make the doorway bigger so that he can get in. He's broken my arm chair by sitting in it, and he has to sleep on the floor as the bed isn't long enough. It's all on account of your tonic, ma'am, and you'll have to do something about it."

"You must have given him too much," said the old woman.

"Well, even if I did, you should have warned me that it would turn him into a monster!" screamed the Mountainy Woman. "We're ashamed to let the neighbors see him, for fear they'll think he's not our son, but a Changeling, and if he grows for the next four or five years he'll have to build a barn to sleep in. I wanted a tall lad, but nothing like Big William!"

"You're an ill-natured, discontented woman," cried the old woman. "Serves you right for not following my instructions. So your son is like a Changeling, is he? Shame on you!"

And the old woman stalked into the stone hut and banged the door.

"Changeling, indeed!" she cried. Then she stood looking at the Lop-eared Creature, perched on its stool blinking at her. "Changeling indeed?" she said, much more slowly, and then, "Changeling—indeed!" more slowly still, and she began to chuckle.

"Give me some more tea," said the Lop-eared Creature shrilly. "And some bread. I'm hungry."

"You're four feet tall, as ugly as a yellow toad, and over five hundred years old," said the old woman. "Well, well, well."

The next morning, long before his parents were up, Big William was sitting on the wall of the poultry yard and sadly watching the sun rise over the mountains. His mother had come home the night before in such a temper that she had thrown a sod of turf at him. Big William's feelings were hurt, because he loved his mother.

"Good morning, Big William," said a shrill voice, suddenly. "You couldn't jump as far as I could, for all your size."

Big William gazed in amazement at the oddest little creature that he had ever seen. It had a wrinkled yellow face, long floppy ears, and its crooked, skinny body was clothed in a brown leather suit much too big for it. It gave a huge leap down the rough mountain side.

"Come on, jump!" it cried.

"I can do that easily," cried Big William, and he took a flying leap after the Lop-eared Creature.

"Well, you can't run as fast as I can," cried the Creature, "in spite of your long legs."

"Maybe I can," said Big William.

"Then catch me," screamed the Lop-eared Creature, and

away it went, with Big William pounding after it. They ran for miles, until the boy was so exhausted that he had to give up—and in a flash the Creature had vanished. And there was poor Big William, completely lost in the heart of the Sperrin Mountains, without an idea which way to turn.

He wandered about, trying to find a path, and finally he came to the old woman's stone hut, which was nearby. He knocked at the door, was told to come in, and by stooping, and pushing, he just managed to squeeze into the kitchen. The old woman was sitting, weaving tweed, and she just kept working while she looked Big William over, from the top of his fine dark head to his patched and worn boots.

"A fine tall man, William," she commented. "Not a monster at all, and nothing to be ashamed of. Your parents should be glad to have you."

"That's all very well, ma'am," said Big William, astonished that she seemed to know him. "But suppose I grow any bigger? My parents are poor sheep farmers, and they have to get my clothes and boots made specially. Besides, I eat a terrible lot."

"There's fresh milk and griddle bread on the table," said the old woman. "You need your breakfast, boy. And while you eat, watch how I make this beautiful cloth. How would you like to learn to make tweed, too? Stay a few days and I'll teach you, and then you can practice, and you'll soon have a trade that will help to support your parents."

"But they don't know I'm here," protested Big William.

"Your mother won't be lonely," said the old woman soothingly. "I've made sure of that."

No, the Mountainy Woman was certainly not lonely! She got up that morning and made the breakfast and then——

"Good morning, mother dear," came a shrill voice from

the heap of blankets where Big William slept. "Is the porridge ready? I'm hungry." And the Lop-eared Creature
hopped out of the blankets and ran to the Mountainy
Woman.

"Go away, you ugly thing," screamed the Mountainy
Woman. "What are you doing in William's bed?"

"But I'm William, your son," cried the Creature, and it
tried to hide its yellow head and floppy ears under the
Mountainy Woman's apron.

With a scream of terror she ran out of the door and found
her husband in the shed splitting wood. He hurried back
with her and they found the Lop-eared Creature scraping
out of the porridge pot.

"I was so hungry, dear parents," it squeaked. "I've eaten
it all."

The Mountainy Man made for it with his stick, but
whenever he struck the Creature was always someplace
else.

"Don't strike me, Dad," it wailed. "I'm William."

"You're not!" cried the Mountainy Woman and she
rushed from the house to look for her son. She and her
husband searched in the mountains all day, and in the
evening they were forced to go home. The Lop-eared
Creature was in the kitchen stirring a pot, from which came
a delicious smell of chicken soup.

"I've cooked three or four," it said. "I'm sure you're very
hungry."

"My good laying pullets!" cried the Mountainy Woman.
"You robber! I couldn't touch a bite."

While they watched in horror, the Creature drank all the
soup and picked the four chickens to the bones.

"Shall we have some lamb tomorrow, Dad?" it suggested.

For the next few days the Mountainy Man spent his time

guarding his sheep from the Lop-eared Creature, and the Mountainy Woman took to her bed and refused to eat. On the fourth day the Creature boiled two eggs and made toast and brought this to her in the bedroom.

"Dear mother, don't starve," it pleaded.

But the Mountainy Woman went right under the bedclothes and wept.

The Lop-eared Creature ate the eggs and toast itself, but it shook its head until its ears flapped. It wasn't really a cruel creature, and it decided things had gone far enough.

Next morning the Mountainy Woman was awakened by the sound of Big William's voice in the kitchen.

"Mother," he called. "See what a lovely length of tweed I've made all by myself. Enough for a new suit. And I'm going to make tweed always now, and pay you back for all your kindness."

Well, the Mountainy Woman and the Mountainy Man hugged their son again and again.

"To think that I called you a monster," sobbed the Mountainy Woman.

"To think that I was ashamed to walk beside the seven feet of you, or grudged you your fill of food," choked the Mountainy Man. "You can grow as big as a house if you like."

"Well, that would be a bit too big," said Big William. "I'll be all right if I stay as I am."

And the funny thing was that he did. Seven feet he was and seven feet he stayed, and was soon famous over the countryside as the maker of the best handwoven tweed ever seen in those parts. For Big William visited the old woman again, and learned from her many secrets of blending dyes, and of intricate weaving.

Usually the Lop-eared Creature was there, eating griddle

bread and drinking strong tea. But there was always a glass of milk specially for William. Unknown to him, the old woman used to pour a few drops of something into it, to keep him from growing any more. It was just as well that she did so—because Big William would have been growing still.

3

The Wise Woman

THERE WAS ONCE A WISE WOMAN WHO HAD SO MUCH wisdom that she didn't know what to do with it, and indeed it was useless to her for it was so jumbled up in her head that she never knew where to find what she needed. If somebody asked her how to cure a sick puppy she might tell him how many mountains there were on the moon. Once when a woman asked her for a few hints on butter-making, the Wise Woman announced that she had known a leprechaun to use up three million, two hundred thousand, six hundred and fifty-nine nails in one night's hammering!

So the people stopped going to her for advice. Then the poor Wise Woman tried to sort out her wisdom and tidy it, but there was always too much new wisdom pouring into her mind.

Now the reason for this was that near her little house was a wishing well, a beautiful little spring bubbling up out of the rock and shaded by willow bushes. The Wise Woman drank the spring water every day, and as her first thought was always to want more wisdom she got more and more of it—faster than she could deal with it—and so she was never really any better off.

On a certain lovely sunny morning the Wise Woman stood at her door and watched the smoke rising from a little cottage at the far side of the valley. A young farm laborer and his wife lived there.

"Trouble brewing there!" The thought popped into the Wise Woman's head without asking her if she wanted it. "A decent young couple, too, even if they are a bit empty-headed and lazy, but, I'm thinking before long——" She didn't even finish thinking it out, because the number of redheaded people in the city of Dublin popped up in her mind instead, and so confused her that she forgot what she wanted to know.

The farm laborer was late arriving at work that day, and the farmer was already hard at work turning the hay to the warm sun.

"It's nice to see you," he said sarcastically. "I hope you had a good sleep and didn't rush too much over your breakfast."

"It's a good stretch up from our place," growled the young man, taking his fork and working off down the field away from his master. The farmer was working faster and soon overtook him.

"I like to see a lad with energy," said the farmer with a snigger. "If you worked just a bit slower you might be able to toss next year's hay as well as this year's."

"That's very clever," snapped the young man.

"Try getting out at the *other* side of the bed tomorrow," said the farmer. "They say everything has a right side and a wrong side."

"If I had my wish," growled the young man, "I wouldn't do one more day's work here."

"That's easy. You've got your wish," laughed the farmer. "And I'm delighted to give it to you, for my shadow makes a better shape at working than you do."

When the young man realized that he had lost his job he begged the farmer to keep him on, but in vain. When evening came there was nothing for it but to go home and tell his wife about it. The young woman talked until her tongue was tired, and then cried until her eyes were tired, and then started talking again.

"We're going to the Wise Woman first thing tomorrow," she said. "I'm thinking we could do with a bit of wisdom."

The next morning they set out and tramped across the valley. The way was long and the sun hot and they were tired and thirsty, but near the Wise Woman's little house they saw just what they wanted—a clear spring bubbling from a rock and shaded by willow bushes. They drank the delicious cool water and threw themselves on the grass to rest.

"I wish I were a dog, then I'd have four legs instead of two——" began the young man.

"I'd rather have wings and fly," interrupted his wife. "I wish I were a lark."

The wishing well was about the strongest of its kind in the country. It could do practically anything, and very quickly, too.

A moment later a very shaggy dog was dashing about barking, and a terrified lark was soaring and screaming into the sky. Such a fuss they made. The Wise Woman dashed out of her cottage, and because she was so wise she knew at once what was wrong. But the cure for the trouble had got lost under a heap of other wisdom.

How she searched for it! But she only found the reason why the tide comes in and out, and where the best blackberries would grow next year. And while she was rummaging through all this useless knowledge the Lark and the Shaggy Dog had gone barking and screaming out of sight.

How unhappy they were! But when night fell, and the Lark came down to the earth once more, they made a wonderful discovery. They understood each other's language quite well and could talk freely.

"Oh, what are we to do now?" twittered the poor Lark. "It's just dreadful to be a bird, and see you such an ugly dog."

"Of course," growled the Dog. "But it can't last forever. I've heard tell that a year and a day after a human being has been changed into something else is the day on which he has a good chance of getting back to his own shape. When our day comes round we must make sure to be at the wishing well. That water has changed us, and it can just as easily change us back again."

"Yes," trilled the Lark, "and until then we must keep together, no matter what happens to us. A year and a day is such a long, long time to wait."

Well, it was indeed a long time, and not an easy time for the Dog and the Lark, but at last their great day came round. And on that same day, little guessing how important it was, the Wise Woman was sitting in her kitchen drinking a cup of strong tea, brewed from well water.

But suddenly she put down the cup and went to the door. Her wisdom said that someone needed her help. But who?

And where? She could not find that bit of knowledge, only the place where the largest diamond in the world was hidden—and the best way to treat a bee sting.

"Dear me," sighed the Wise Woman. "This is really *most* annoying."

And at that very moment the Dog and the Lark were under the willow trees drinking and wishing. Then they waited, watching one another carefully, and nothing happened!

"What's wrong?" twittered the Lark. "I knew that you would wish for our release, so I wished that our cottage would be safe and sound after all this time."

The Dog howled and ran round in circles. "Ow, ooow," he yelped. "I left our change-back to *you*. I wanted to make sure I'd get my job again. Oooow!" How the Dog did howl and wail, and the Wise Woman, standing at her door and thinking as hard as she could, knew without a doubt that— there were seventy-nine caterpillars on the biggest ragweed plant in the valley.

"This is awful altogether!" cried the poor Wise Woman. "Was there ever such an unhappy creature in Ireland?" and she went into her kitchen and poured herself another cup of tea. Now the water from the wishing well was twice as strong when it was boiled, and four times as strong now that it had stewed itself black. There was almost unlimited power in that cup of tea!

"That's as fine a drop of tea as ever I tasted," said the Wise Woman. "And, indeed, I need it, poor moithered creature that I am. I wish—indeed and indeed, I wish I could get things straight in my head."

The cup dropped from her hand and smashed on the hearth. A great blackness came before her eyes, and there was a fluttering and then a great crash in her head as all her knowledge sorted itself out and dropped into place. In a flash she could see everything clearly, and the first thing that jumped to the front of her mind was the whole story of the Lark and the Dog and their wasted wishes.

"The creatures!" she cried. "Ah, the poor creatures," and she dashed to the door. "Come in, Lark, come in, Dog, my poor neighbors. To think that I didn't recognize you. Now don't mind how you look, come right in. Sure I'm your friend."

The Dog paused on the doorstep, his tail down, his ears drooping, but the Lark fluttered timidly in and perched on the dresser, still softly sobbing.

"You must drink a drop of tea, dear neighbors," said the Wise Woman, for now she saw that if they drank the strong tea and wished again they had another chance of saving themselves. But *all* the laws of magic forbade that she should tell them what they must do.

The Lark was sobbing too much to want tea, and she tried to tell this to the Wise Woman who was pouring it out into two bowls. But the Wise Woman pretended not to understand, so the Lark gulped down a few drops rather than offend her. The Dog hesitated, and then crawled into the kitchen on his stomach and lapped the tea politely.

"Now if only, if only they would wish quickly," thought the Wise Woman, and she had to bite her lips to stop herself from telling them to do so.

"I wish you good health, ma'am," said the Lark to her. "You're really very kind."

The Wise Woman wrung her hands. That was the Lark's wish wasted! She turned to the Dog.

The Dog, however, simply could not endure this tea-drinking and conversation. He would thank the Wise Woman, who could not, indeed, be very wise at all, for she was giving them no help. Yes, he would thank her and wish her a very good day——

The Wise Woman felt the words coming. She must stop them! She *must*. She drew back her strong, bony old foot, and the Dog landed, yelping with rage and pain, outside the door. He hurled himself against it as it slammed.

How he wished that he were a man! How he wished that he and his wife were freed of the spell and that the old woman were—— His wish broke off, just in time, as he heard his wife call out in her old familiar voice. He answered and it was no longer a bark! They were free!

But the Wise Woman was still breathless at her narrow escape. If the young man had finished his wish he would have turned her into a cat.

"Oh, my goodness," she whispered. "But I suppose all is well if it ends well. Still—a cat. Ah dear me!"

Then she realized that the two young people were still there, stammering out thanks, and apologies, and promises to be sensible as long as they lived.

"Ah, go on home," said the good-natured old woman. "You've got your first wishes as well. The cottage is just as you left it, and I'm thinking that the farmer is tired of telling his shadow to toss hay. Go on along to him, say you're sorry, and he'll take you back. And, indeed, it's more than you deserve. A cat, indeed!" and the Wise Woman began to chuckle and shake, and as the happy young people hurried off she hugged herself with glee. She had suddenly realized that now that she had got all her wisdom sorted out, she was the wisest old woman in the whole of Ireland.

4

Fergus Og and the Foreign Witch

IF THERE HAD NOT BEEN A THUNDERSTORM THAT AFTERNOON in the Glebe Hills there would have been no story to tell. Katey Maloney would not have sheltered under the hedge, but would have gone straight home with the sticks she had gathered. The Foreign Witch would have passed harmlessly overhead, on her way back to her home, in one of the deepest, darkest forests on the continent of Europe—and Fergus Og, the lord of the Fairy Fort would not have had a visitor.

But there *was* a thunderstorm, and Katey Maloney sheltered under the hedge until it had passed. When the clouds had rolled away and the rain stopped she came out from her hiding place and hurried across the big field past the Fort, dragging her bundle of sticks after her. And there, in the wet grass, she saw a very strange thing. She saw a broom handle, with a few smouldering twigs at the end of it.

"That's a very queer thing," said Katey to herself. "Someone has burned the head off his brush. Looks as if he'd been poking the fire with it. I wonder why?"

And Katey picked up the handle and rubbed the burning part of it in the wet grass until it stopped smoking. "Well," she said. "It doesn't look as if anybody wants it, so I might as well take it with me. Maybe Ma would use it for beating the mats."

And off she went, down the hillside, taking the broom handle with her.

At the very same minute the Foreign Witch was standing outside the Fort, wondering who lived there. She walked round it three times before she noticed that there was a heavy wooden door hidden between two great rocks. First she rapped on the door with her knuckles, and then, because she was a very ill-tempered person, she kicked at it with her great ugly foot. She kicked so hard that she hurt her toes, and when Fergus Og and the Gentle People of the Fort came to the door, they found the Witch dancing about with rage and making horrible faces.

The Gentle People simply did not know what to make of her. They were all tall and beautiful—the real people of the Ever Young. They were shy, and seldom left their Fort. Sometimes Fergus Og, their leader, visited the Leprechaun who lived in the thorn tree in the Fort Field. And sometimes a wandering Banshee dropped in for a meal and gossiped about the outer world. But they could not remember having heard of anybody quite as ugly, as evil, and as horrible as the Foreign Witch.

Fergus Og asked politely what she wanted, but she

could not understand. She shouted something in her own language, and he could not understand her. So they tried the international speech of all magical peoples, and the Foreign Witch explained that she had been flying over the Glebe Hills, on her way back from a Witches' Conference, that had been held in the forests of Canada.

"And then a great flash of lightning came and burned all the twigs from my broom," she shouted. "A nice state of affairs."

"So you had to land, poor thing," said Fergus Og.

"Yes, indeed," snarled the Witch. "And my broom is ruined. How dare you let your lightning destroy my broom!"

"Madam," protested Fergus Og, "I have no power over the clouds. But since you came to my Fort for aid I will do all that I can for you. And you will be my guest until you can leave for your own land."

And the Gentle People made a meal for the Witch and waited on her hand and foot.

That evening the Leprechaun of the Fort Field was suprised by a visit from Fergus Og.

"Come in, My Lord. Welcome to my tree," cried the little fellow, bowing until his beard swept the ground.

"I need your help, Leprechaun," said Fergus Og, and he explained about the Foreign Witch. "I have searched the field for the damaged broomstick, but I cannot find it anywhere," he said.

"And how could you," snapped the Leprechaun. "Hasn't me fine Katey Maloney taken it off home with her! But haven't you told your visitor that there are plenty of grand ragweed plants in the field? What more does she need?"

"Alas," said Fergus Og, "she will not ride on them. In her country it is not done. Here, we ride on ragweed. In her land they use broomsticks, and she tells me that in Eastern Lands the people fly on magic carpets. Since her broom has been taken away you must get another one."

"Who? Me?" squeaked the Leprechaun.

"Yes, you!" said Fergus Og, and the Leprechaun could only bow his head and obey.

Early the next morning Katey Maloney's mother was sweeping her garden path with her yard brush. She was in a very bad temper. Things had been going badly in the house ever since the day before. She had tripped twice over the odd stick that Katey had brought home, and had dropped a bowl of soup when the same stick had clattered suddenly to the ground in the corner, where she had left it leaning against the wall. Now, as she swept, she heard another crash in the kitchen. She dropped the yard brush and ran in.

"I—I—I tripped over that stick, and I've broken a jug," wailed Katey.

"Bad luck to it for a stick," cried Mrs. Maloney. "I'll break it up and burn it, so I will." She went out to fetch her brush to sweep up the pieces of the jug, but the brush was not to be found. She and Katey searched, but in vain, and this was not strange because the Leprechaun was dragging it through the fields to the Fort.

The Gentle People were delighted to see him, for they were thoroughly tired of the Foreign Witch. But when the Witch saw the yard brush she shook her head from side to side.

"I won't ride on a dirty old brush like that," she said. "Our brooms are for indoor cleaning only." And she leaned back, folded her ugly hands over her stomach and prepared to go to sleep. "You can wake me in another hour for a meal," she told the Gentle People, who were far too courteous to be rude to a guest.

"You must put that brush back" said Fergus Og to the Leprechaun, "and try to get something better, otherwise we will never get rid of her."

The Leprechaun grumbled a lot about "people who are never satisfied," but he went off obediently, and left the yard brush at Mrs. Maloney's back door. He could see, through the door, that there was rather a lot of smoke in the kitchen. The chimney did not seem to be drawing well at all.

"Well, we all have our troubles," he sighed, and he went off to try to think of a plan to get the Foreign Witch started on her homeward journey.

Late that evening the Leprechaun arrived back at the Fort, hot and breathless, and this time he was dragging a length of piping that he had taken from the roadside, where some workmen were mending the drains.

The Foreign Witch had just finished her supper. She leaned back in her chair, smacking her lips, and glared at the pipe.

"What's that for?" she demanded.

"All modern indoor cleaning is done by sucking dirt up through a pipe," said the Leprechaun. "It's done by electricity, so if we could get some lightning———"

"Don't talk to me about lightning," snarled the Witch. "I've had enough to do with lightning—and I've had enough of you and your silly ideas. If you can't get me a decent broom to ride on I'll stay here for ever."

The Gentle People gasped with horror. A guest could never be turned away, but if this horrible person stayed for ever———!

"You must put that pipe back where it belongs," said Fergus Og, to the Leprechaun. "Bring the lady's own broomstick, and we will put new twigs in it."

How the little fellow grumbled, but he went off obediently, dragging the drainpipe behind him. As for the Foreign Witch, she sat and laughed.

"Ha, ha, ha, HA!" she cackled, because she was enjoying her stay in the Fort, and she knew, because she had magical powers of knowing things, that the Leprechaun would *not* be able to bring her own broomstick. She knew that Katey Maloney's mother had chopped it up and burned it, and that it was the evil in the broomstick that had choked the chimney and caused it to smoke.

"Yes, bring my stick and have it mended," she chuckled. "Ho, ho, ho, HO!"

Well, Mrs. Maloney had done everything she could think of to make the chimney draw, and finally she sent for the sweep. Early the next day he arrived and went to work.

"Oh, it's very badly blocked, ma'am," he said, and he had to push with all his might to get his brush up the chimney. The evil that had come from the broomstick made it as difficult as possible, but at last the sweep said, "Ah, that's done it!" and began to pull his brush down again. It came down very easily, and as he pulled he screwed off his poles and laid them aside. At last he brought down the pole next to the one with the big round sweep's brush on it, and then he gasped. For the last one and the brush were not there.

The sweep went outside and looked up at the chimney, but there was no sign of his brush. Then he went in and poked up the chimney again, but the chimney was quite clear.

"Where's it gone to?" demanded the sweep, but neither Katey nor her mother could answer him.

The Leprechaun could have answered, but he was already halfway up to the Fort with the sweep's brush.

Fergus Og was watching for him at the door between the rocks.

"Well?" he demanded.

"This is the finest sweeping brush in Ireland," declared the Leprechaun. "And not only that, it has the soot from the burning of the Foreign Witch's broomstick in it."

Well, the Witch had made up her mind to stay much longer in the Fort, because she was simply having the time of her life. But when she saw the big brush, with its fine bamboo handle, and the evil magic of her own stick clinging to it—well, she couldn't resist it. In fact, she had never seen anything that she liked better, and she was suddenly in a dreadful hurry to get home to her forest and show off before the other witches. She didn't even thank the Gentle People for their kindness. She just snatched the sweep's brush, dashed out of the Fort, and went sailing away.

"Thank you, good Leprechaun," said Fergus Og. "You have saved us from a most dreadful situation."

"Only too pleased to oblige, sir," said the Leprechaun, and he hopped off back to his tree. As for Fergus Og, he closed the door of his Fort, and neither he nor any of the Gentle People have come out since that day.

Katey and her Mother never had any more trouble with the chimney, but the sweep still wonders where his brush has gone. But he does not worry, because he has had a run of the most wonderful good luck. He does not know that before the door of the Fort closed, Fergus Og, who is ever just and courteous, blew a breath of good luck to him down the wind, to make up to him for the loss of his brush.

5

Barney O'Dowd's Dragon

THIS ALL HAPPENED VERY MANY YEARS AGO, BUT THE
people of the district still talk about Barney O'Dowd's
Dragon.

Barney lived with his daughter, Nora, and if the Dragon
is still remembered so is Nora's embroidery, or "flowering"
as it used to be called. All the women and girls did flowering, stitching flowers on the fine linen handkerchiefs that
were woven down in the mill in the village. They used to sit
in little groups outside the cottages, sewing and chattering,
and very often they spoke of Nora O'Dowd who was the
best flowerer in the whole countryside.

"The Wee Folk must help her with it," they used to say.
"That's why she never does her sewing here with us, but
slips away up to the Fairy Fort. No human fingers could

stitch such flowers—why you'd think they would fall right off the linen, they look so real."

"Aye, there's magic in it," the women decided. "That stupid Barney O'Dowd's daughter couldn't do such flowering unless she were helped with it!"

Well, there was magic in the air up around the Fairy Fort, sure enough, but Nora did her sewing all herself. She didn't like to sit with the other women and girls, because she knew they were jealous of her, so she would pack her sewing into a basket, with some soda bread for her lunch, and when Barney went off in the mornings to the nearby farm, where he worked as a laborer, Nora would go away up to the Fort and spend the day there. She wasn't afraid of the Wee People at all, in fact she sometimes used to wish that they would take her into Tir na nOg just for an adventure. Sometimes she got so tired of just sitting sewing that she was quite discontented.

"I'm so tired of these old flowers," she said aloud, one lovely evening, as she sat under the twisted thorn tree on the side of the Fort. "I wish I had real flowers instead of these silken ones."

And as she spoke the red rose that she had just embroidered rolled off the linen and lay in her lap, as real as any rose had ever been.

"Oh!" Nora looked up into the thorn tree and wagged her finger at it. "That was a good joke to play on me," she said. "Thank you. It's a beautiful rose, and smells just lovely."

Nora held the rose against her face, and then pinned it on her dress. It would be a good story to tell her father when she got home. She wound up her threads and reached for her basket. But now she really got a shock, for the flowers had fallen from *all* the sewing in her basket, too. It was full of the most beautiful blooms, but the linen squares were as plain as when they had come from the mill!

When Barney got home from work he found the kitchen simply full of flowers, and his daughter rushing here and there filling jam jars and old tins with water to put them in.

"Where in the world did you get those?" Barney demanded.

"My flowering came alive," explained Nora. "And all that I had in the house, too! I haven't a stitch to take down to the mill, but the flowers are lovely, and I'll start sewing and work twice as hard."

"I don't believe such silly talk," snapped Barney. "Came alive, indeed! What you mean is that you exchanged your good sewing with someone for a few armfuls of flowers that will be withered in a few days. That won't pay the rent, Nora, so you'd better get to work and never be so foolish again."

"I'm telling you the truth," said Nora. "You needn't believe me if you don't like," and she held a big bunch of pansies up to her face and sniffed delightedly.

It was a Saturday evening, and on Saturdays Barney, who was a rather vain old fellow, used to tidy himself up and go down to the town. In a few minutes he called his daughter.

"Nora, where's my yellow neckcloth, the one you made for me with the red dragon on it?"

Nora dropped her flowers with a gasp, because a horrible thought had suddenly come to her. "I left it on the bed with your socks," she said, rushing to the bedroom door. Barney was standing there, holding a piece of yellow silk in his hand, but the embroidered dragon had gone.

"Dad," said Nora in a shaking voice, "is the shotgun loaded?"

"Now why——?" began Barney, and just at that minute

they saw the Dragon looking at them from under the bed. "Ow!" yelled Barney, and sprang on to the bed, boots and all. Nora grabbed a sweeping brush, and the Dragon gave a snort of smoke and flames and dived in out of sight.

"Now, do you believe that my sewing has come to life?" cried Nora.

"No, I don't believe it," quavered Barney. "I haven't tasted a drop of drink this week, but I'm imagining things. Still, if there's some sort of an animal under the bed, girl, don't go for it with the brush. If you make it angry it'll attack us."

The Dragon had no intention of attacking them. It was very timid, and finally Nora had to entice it with a saucer of milk before it would come from under the bed. As it was lapping the milk, with its long forked tongue, they had a chance of looking at it, from the top of its ugly head to the end of its long scaley tail. It was red, as the embroidered dragon had been, but it was about six feet long, and it breathed out smoke in a most frightening manner.

"But I don't believe it's fierce at all," said Nora. "Will you get down off that bed, Dad, before you destroy it completely."

"There are no such things as dragons," said Barney. "But we'll have to chase this thing away. Shoo, there, shoo!"

The Dragon didn't shoo. It looked at Barney with big, red reproachful eyes. It belonged to him, having come from his neckcloth, and it intended to be faithful. It rubbed itself against his leg, as a cat will do, and the armored scales on its back were so sharp that poor Barney yelled, and would have jumped on the bed again had not Nora grabbed his arm.

"He's a lovely Dragon, Dad," she exclaimed. "Don't be so cross. The poor beast can't understand."

"But what are we to do?" yelled Barney. "People just don't *have* pet dragons!"

"Well, we have one," said Nora.

At first they were able to keep their Dragon a secret, because it was far too timid to leave the cottage. By the time the Dragon had burned the leg off the kitchen table, and scorched one of Barney's shirts that was hanging over a chair to air, it learned to control its breath to a harmless smoking, and only snorted out flames to help Nora kindle the fire. It got on very well with Nora, but it was her father that it loved. It felt that it was Barney's Dragon, and it would watch anxiously for him to come from work each evening. One night Barney dreamed that he was fighting a knight in full armor, and woke to find that the Dragon had got into bed with him and was trying to snuggle against him! Next morning, sleepless and furious, he turned on Nora.

"It must go! I won't have it here!" he stormed.

"But where?" asked his daughter. "We can't put a notice in the post office window—'Nice home wanted for friendly Dragon.' And the poor thing simply loves you, Dad."

That morning the Dragon went with Barney to his work. It wouldn't go home when Barney yelled at it, and at last, in exasperation, he bolted it into one of the outhouses at the farm. Well, he hadn't been more than ten minutes in the field where he was working when the Dragon came up to him, waddling as fast as its legs would let it. The trouble was that there was no longer a door on the outhouse, because the Dragon had burned it off in order to reach its beloved Master.

The farmer was furious! He said that if people kept wild animals as pets they should stay at home with them—and Barney was sacked from that day. Nor would he get any

pay for his work, for that would go to pay for a new door.

Poor Barney took his Dragon home, and found Nora in a kitchen filled with beautiful flowers.

"It's no good, Dad," she cried. "They stay on the linen until I've snipped the last thread, and then off they come."

"I've had enough of this nonsense," cried Barney. "This magic business must quit! Neither of us is earning any money and there's rent owing. What am I to say to the collector when he comes?"

As it happened he didn't have to say anything to the rent collector, because when the man arrived next day the Dragon was in the front garden neatly burning out the weeds without hurting the plants. The rent collector ran for his life and went to the police, saying that the beast must be taken to the Zoo.

When the police sergeant somewhat reluctantly called at O'Dowd's, Barney was making a cup of tea. He had run out of firing, but the Dragon was bringing the kettle to the boil for him. The sergeant bravely stood his ground.

"There are serious charges against you, Barney O'Dowd," he began, and at that the faithful Dragon turned round and said, "Grr-rr-rr," and the sergeant decided that he couldn't be expected to carry out his duty without the aid of the fire brigade.

Next day Nora told the Dragon to come with her and marched off to the Fairy Fort. She stood under the twisted thorn and knocked on it with a stick.

"Listen, You of the Thorn Tree," she said. "You started all this, and it's not a joke any more."

"Well," said a cracked voice from the trunk of the tree, "you wanted a bit of change. You found life dull, didn't you?"

And the Person in the tree began to snigger rudely. The

Dragon wasn't standing for this rudeness to his mistress. He let out an angry snort, and about half of the branches of the tree shrivelled away before his fiery breath.

"Stop," cried the Person in the tree. "Maybe we can come to some sort of agreement after all, Nora O'Dowd. But get your pet to stop destroying my house."

"First of all," said Nora, "you must let my flowering stay on the linen, or I'll never make another penny. And then I beg the protection of the Fairy Fort for our Dragon. The police will shoot him or send him to the Zoo, and sure isn't the creature a fairy dragon after all. Doesn't he belong to your people?"

"Well, there's something in what you say, Nora," said the voice. "But you'll have to wait while I ask the rest of the people of the Fort."

"We'll wait," said Nora, "but hurry, or we'll burn off the rest of your tree."

Well, of course, the Person bestirred himself at that, and it was soon all arranged. The Dragon was to live in the Fort, deep under the earth, but when Nora went there to do her flowering he could creep out and lie at her feet. Well, if Nora's sewing had been beautiful before, it was almost magical now, and she could get so much done that Barney didn't have to go back to work with the farmer at all. He was getting old, so it was time for him to stop work and smoke his pipe by his own fireside.

But for all his talk about how glad he was that the Dragon was gone, he seemed to spend a lot of his time, not at his fireside, but smoking his pipe up at the Fairy Fort. And when he bought tobacco he never seemed to need to buy any matches. A pet Dragon has its uses!

6

The Ugly Person and the Curranty Bread

THE PEOPLE WHO LIVED IN THE HILLS BEYOND BALLYFAY seldom went into the town, because they could buy almost anything from Davey the Dealer's cart. You could buy a broomstick from Davey or a stick of barley-sugar—a suit of secondhand clothes—a cough bottle or a mousetrap. Or if you wanted something special Davey would fetch it, and he took payment in fresh eggs and butter, homespun, fruit, or vegetables.

He took six dozen fine duck eggs from old Ellen Teggarty in exchange for a big flat-bottomed, flat-lidded black baking pot. As a rule Ellen's sister Peggy did the bargaining with Davey. She knew that Davey was greedy, and she refused to part with her eggs unless she got value for them. But on this particular morning Peggy was spreading her washing on the hillside, and when she came down Davey was gone and Ellen was carrying the black pot.

"What ever is that?" Peggy asked.

"It's a baking pot," said Ellen. "I'm going to bake bread the way mother used to do in the old days—with the hot turf under the pot and spread on the lid."

"Was it from Davey you got it?" said Peggy, looking suspiciously at the pot.

"He went to no end of trouble to get it for me," said Ellen. "I'd been saying one day how tired I was of baker's bread."

"No end of trouble—my foot!" snapped Peggy. "It looks as if he'd picked it off a rubbish dump! And what did you give him for it, if I may make so bold as to ask?"

"Just six dozen eggs," muttered Ellen, "and cheap at that."

But Peggy threw up her hands in horror. "Ach, you foolish old woman," she cried. "Six dozen of our lovely eggs, and nothing in exchange but a dirty old pot! No tea or sugar! Just an empty pot—and we needing groceries!"

As it happened, the pot was not empty at all. The sisters saw nothing but dust, because the Person who lived in the pot was invisible. He was not a Leprechaun nor a Lochrieman, nor any of the respectable fairy races. He was so ugly, so hairy and wrinkled that they had refused to have anything to do with him. So he had taken to living in the pot, and made himself invisible every time the lid was lifted, which wasn't often, because the pot had sat for ages at the very back of a secondhand shop, until Davey the Dealer had bought it for one and ninepence. He had made a very satisfactory deal with Ellen, and at that very minute he was driving up into the hills, with the six dozen duck eggs, and laughing to himself.

"Just you wait, Peggy, until I'm lifting a lovely big round cake of curranty soda bread out of my pot!" said Ellen, and she seized a cloth and soap and began to wash out the dust.

The Ugly Person, invisible as he was, hopped hastily out, climbed up to the top of the grandfather clock, and made horrible faces at Ellen. Fortunately, she could not see them, because the Ugly Person was bad enough when he was pleased, but when he made faces he was simply dreadful. He watched furiously while Ellen scoured out his pot, and as soon as she had finished he hopped back into it again. It was still rather damp, but the Ugly Person curled up in it, shivering, and finally sneezed and went asleep.

"Have you caught cold, Sister?" asked Ellen, who was by this time measuring out her flour.

"Certainly not," snapped Peggy. "Just because *you* sneezed doesn't mean that *I* have a cold. It's the dust from your precious pot, so it is."

"I didn't sneeze," said Ellen. "*You* did."

"You've gone daft," said Peggy. "Nobody in her senses would have given six dozen lovely big green eggs for a bit of rubbish. Just wait until I see Davey the Dealer. I'll have something to say to him, so I will!"

"You'll see if I'm daft when you're eating my fresh curranty bread," said Ellen. "There, you really did sneeze that time!"

The Ugly Person had sneezed in his sleep, and the two old women had jumped at the sudden sound.

"If you ask me," said Peggy, "I'd say your black pot isn't lucky in the house. It's making us imagine things, so it is!"

"My bread won't be an imagination," chuckled Ellen, and she threw fresh sods on the fire. "Away you out and look for eggs and leave me to my baking."

Well, Ellen made her dough, and put a whole pound of

currants in it. Then she pulled out glowing turf and made a nice, flat resting place for the black pot. Then—into the pot went the big round cake of dough, and on went the lid, weighed down with more glowing sods.

"This is going to be the finest cake of bread that was ever baked," declared Ellen to herself.

It looked as if she might be right, because when Peggy came back the bread was rising so well that it was pushing the lid up from the pot.

"See that now," said Ellen. "And doesn't it smell good! Maybe now, Peggy, if you're set against soda bread, I'd better eat it all myself."

"Now Ellen, don't be greedy——" began Peggy, and at that very moment the most extraordinary thing happened. The cake of curranty bread pushed the lid right off the pot, hopped out, and began to dance up and down on the hearth.

"I told you there was something queer about that pot," scolded Peggy. "It's put a *piseog* on the bread."

"Oh, oh, my bread!" wailed Ellen. "It'll be hopping into the fire on me in a minute."

Well, that was not very likely, because the Ugly Person did not want to burn himself. He had been fast asleep when Ellen had put her dough on top of him, and he woke up choking, with dough and currants in his mouth, eyes, nose, and ears, and packed tightly all around him.

He was simply furious! He blew and blew until the cake of bread rose and pushed the lid from the pot, and when he had done his little dance of rage on the hearth he made for the open door to cool himself—for it was a hot job to be baked.

But Ellen wasn't going to stand by and see her curranty bread run away. She seized a long, steel, toasting fork, chased after the bread and stuck the fork firmly into it.

"Got you," she gasped.

The bread went on hopping, and hopped right out into the yard. The Ugly Person was stronger than Ellen, and she found herself pulled along, too.

"I'm not letting go, *piseog* or no *piseog*," she cried, and at that moment the Ugly Person blew so much air into the cake of bread that it sailed up—and up—higher than the cottage, and brought Ellen with it, dangling from the toasting fork.

"Come down out of that," screamed Peggy. "Don't be silly."

"I can't let go or I'll fall," wailed poor Ellen, and the curranty bread floated through the air, down across the field towards the duck pond.

Just at that minute Davey the Dealer's cart appeared over the top of the hill. Davey was driving back after his morning of bargaining, and when he saw Ellen Teggarty sailing along under what looked like a speckled balloon he nearly fell out of his cart with surprise.

"Look out, ma'am, or you'll be in the pond," he shouted.

That was just what the Ugly Person had planned. When he was above the middle of the pond he poked a hole in the curranty bread and crept out, making a great hop into the branches of a tree. The air immediately began to go out of the cake. It sank slowly lower and lower, and the ducks, seeing their mistress coming down into *their* pond from the sky, hurried to the shore, quacking angrily.

"Oh, Ooooooh!" wailed poor Ellen. "Don't drop me into the water. Sure I'll be up to my neck in mud, so I will—and that Davey, that caused all the trouble, watching me, too! Oooh!"

The soda bread now looked like a big flat, airless pancake, but the Ugly Person wanted to torment Ellen a little more before she went into the pond. He let himself become visible, and made his very worst grimace, leaning from the tree to admire his ugly reflection in the water. And then he got such a shock that he nearly fell in himself, for a round, pleasant face was smiling up at him. Being baked in a curranty cake had improved him very much. It had taken the wrinkles and hairiness away, and he was a plump, handsome little fellow now! Poor Ellen's boots were just touching the water when the Person—ugly no longer—blew her to the side of the pond, where she landed quite safely, dropped the toasting fork, and ran into the cottage. The Person was grateful to Ellen for baking him. He jumped from his tree and ran after her—past Peggy who was standing amongst the quacking ducks, watching everything with her mouth wide open.

She was still standing there when Davey the Dealer jumped from his cart and ran into the field.

"That's a right useful sort of balloon your sister was sailing with," said Davey, looking at the speckled pancake, which had folded itself round the toasting fork for all the world like an umbrella when you let it down.

"But it's not a suitable game for an old woman," Davey went on coaxingly. "I could give you a few shillings worth of goods for it and take it off your hands."

"Oh, we wouldn't part with it for anything," said Peggy quickly. "Why shouldn't two old women go sailing? None of the neighbors has anything like this invention."

By this time Davey was simply wild to go sailing. Besides, he told himself, he could find out the secret of the balloon that folded like an umbrella, and could make more and sell them.

"Come on out to the cart, and choose what you'd like in exchange," he pleaded.

And this Peggy did, and she helped herself to far more than the value of the six dozen eggs that Davey had taken from Ellen.

But it served Davey right for being so greedy. He was never able to make a penny out of the remains of Ellen's curranty bread, because the magic had gone out of it, and when he got it into his cart he found that it was only a toasting fork and some half-cooked dough.

Back in the kitchen, Ellen and Peggy had a long chat with the Person, and they came to an agreement. The Person was to live in the pot, because he was fond of it. But when Ellen wanted to bake she was to rap three times on the lid before putting in her dough, because the Person might happen to be invisible at the time, and he didn't want to be baked again!

Many a good cake of curranty bread came out of that pot. Ellen and Peggy ate so much that they got quite fat—but they never forgot to leave a few fresh slices in the pot for the Person who lived there!

7

Timothy
and the Lochrie-Men

IF TIMOTHY THE MILKMAN HAD NOT BEEN SO LAZY ABOUT shaving—or if old Madge Moloney had not let her little black cow graze on the rath of the Lochrie-men—or if Madge had not had rheumatism——? But let's have the story from the beginning!

The little town of Ballymunty stands on the edge of a bog. Timothy delivered milk morning and evening to the people of Ballymunty, driving his pony and cart along the bog road, past Madge Moloney's cottage, and past the rath of the Lochrie-men. Sometimes he would tell of how, after dark, he had seen lights moving about the bog, and heard footsteps and laughter.

"But they don't bother with me, nor I with them," he would say. "I've never seen one of the creatures yet."

Madge Moloney could have told a different tale, for the Lochrie-men were her nearest neighbors, and she had got to know them quite well. She was not a bit surprised when one of them knocked on her cottage door one evening.

"Good evening to you," said Madge, looking him over casually. Lochrie-men are rather taller than other leprechauns. They have very long beards, which shine very brightly as soon as it gets dark, and they wear long, pointed, brown leather caps, that hang down behind them like tails.

"Good evening to yourself, ma'am, stupid woman that you are," said the Lochrie-man.

"Why so?" demanded the old woman.

"Madge Moloney," said the Lochrie-man, "your little black cow has spent the day grazing on our rath!"

"Sure, what harm has the creature done?" asked Madge.

"The cow has done no harm to the rath," he said, "but the rath has done a lot of harm to the cow. You mustn't drink any of her milk, ma'am, for it's bewitched."

"Och, I'm ruined," wailed the old woman. "I haven't another thing in the world but the few hens. What'll I do at all? And nobody to help me. Wisha, wisha!"

The Lochrie-man scratched his long ear thoughtfully. "I tell you what," he said. "Bring us all the milk from your cow, for it won't hurt us to drink it. And we'll dig your little field for you, and plant potatoes, and turnips, and maybe a few beans. How would that do?"

——Well, that was what they did. Every day old Madge left a can of milk at the foot of the rath, and soon the people of Ballymunty used to ask one another how in the world the old woman could grow such fine vegetables.

"And she bent with the rheumatism!" they used to say.

Madge never told who was helping her. She used to chuckle to herself when she saw lights flitting about in her field at night, for she knew that the little men with the shining beards were at work.

But it was Madge's rheumatism that brought about the next bit of trouble. One morning when she delivered the can of milk at the rath she gave a bit of a shout, and one of the Lochrie-men popped out.

"I'm thinking," said old Madge, "it's a cruel walk for me over the bog. How would it be if I got Timothy the Milkman to deliver it?"

"You mustn't tell our business to anyone," said the Lochrie-man.

"Sure, I won't tell him a word," said the old woman. "I'll slip the can into the cart, and I'll get him to shout a greeting from me to your people as he drives past. He's a good-natured man, even if he is a bit untidy-looking. Then when you hear his voice one of you can slip out, without his seeing you, and lift out the can of milk."

"Well, we can try it," said the Lochrie-man.

Next morning when Timothy came near Madge's cottage he saw the old woman standing on the roadside, and stopped to bid her the time of day.

"You're a decent lad, Timothy," said Madge, coming over to him and leaning into the cart. "It's a pity you don't take more care of your looks. Why don't you shave a bit more often—you're awfully whiskery."

Timothy blushed, and in his confusion did not see Madge set the little milk can under the seat. "I shaved not more than five weeks ago," he said. "I'm a busy man. And sure there's nobody at home but the cat, and she doesn't seem to care."

"Tell me now," said Madge. "Will you do something for me? When you're passing the rath will you shout out good-day to the Little People for me? I'm too full of rheumatism to go that way myself. Will you do that to oblige me, Timothy?"

"Sure," said the kindly milkman, and he went on his way. But, unfortunately, by the time he had reached the rath, Timothy was thinking of something else, and forgot all about his promise. So the Lochrie-men in the rath heard no shout, and the can of the little black cow's milk stayed hidden under the seat in the cart.

It was lucky for Timothy's customers that it *was* so far in under the seat, otherwise one or more of them would have had an adventurous time of it. As it was, when Timothy got home the little can was still there.

"That's strange," said Timothy to himself. "I'm sure I didn't leave anybody without milk. I must have filled an extra can this morning." Now it happened that Timothy's big tabby cat had come out to greet him. She smelled the milk in the can and began to purr.

"All right, Puss," said Timothy. "Seeing that it's left over we might as well *both* have a drink." And they did—the cat from a saucer and Timothy from a cup.

In the evening Timothy drove to Ballymunty as usual to deliver milk, and it was growing dark when he started off for home. There were lights flitting about over the bog, but these didn't worry him. What he could not understand was that there seemed to be a sort of brightness travelling along with him, just in front of his face. He didn't like it a bit, and he went faster than usual. And then—and then something hurled out of the darkness, with a flash and actually lit in the cart beside him.

"Ouch!" yelled Timothy, gazing down into two green eyes, above whiskers that shone like two brushfuls of luminous paint. "You scared the life out of me. What are you doing here, Puss, and what have you got on your whiskers?"

"Take me home quickly," said the cat. "The fairy horsemen are chasing me, Master dear!"

When Timothy heard the cat speak he sprang out of the cart, and the cat sprang after him. The pony immediately took fright and ran for his life. But as his hoof beats clattered away Timothy could hear more hooves clattering on the road towards them.

"I'm dreaming," gasped Timothy. "Cats don't talk."

"Will you stop blathering there and run," cried the cat. "Can't you understand that we're being chased, and that every bit of whisker on your face is shining the same as mine. You're like a beacon! Run, can't you. Run!"

Timothy ran. It was useless to ask questions when one was being chased by horsemen that one could only hear and not see. He dashed wildly across the bog with the cat bounding at his heels.

"They're catching us. Quick, behind this turf stack, and hide your face," ordered the cat.

Timothy wasn't slow to follow this advice, and as he lay trembling behind the turf stack the mysterious hooves went thundering past and away across the bog.

"That was a near shave," said the cat.

Timothy scrambled up onto his knees. "Listen," he said. "I don't understand all this!" And just then he caught sight of his face, which was reflected in a bog hole that was alongside the turf stack. Every hair of his five weeks growth of beard was shining just as brightly as the cat's whiskers! "What's wrong with us?" cried poor Timothy. "What's happening on the bog tonight?"

It didn't take them long to find the answer to that, because from behind the turf stack they saw—what nobody had ever yet seen—they saw the game of hide-and-seek that the Lochrie-men have been playing for hundreds of years with the horsemen of Tir na nOg! The point of the game was that the horsemen hunted the Lochrie-men down, following the bright lights that flashed from the little men's shining beards. What they would have done with them, had they caught them, nobody knows—because they never did catch them. The Lochrie-men were too clever, and they had a trick of whipping off their long leather caps, and pulling them up over their beards, whenever the hoof beats were getting uncomfortably close. This made them invisible at once, and the riders would pass them by. Then the Lochrie-men would laugh, put on their caps again, and go scurrying off.

Well, it was so exciting to watch, that Timothy completely forgot himself. "Well done yourself!" he screamed, as one of the little men escaped in the very instant of capture. And Timothy stood right up in his excitement! Of course, the light from his own face gave him away at once, and the invisible rider swung around and came thundering towards them.

"You idiot!" screamed the cat, and she and Timothy had to run again. This time they finished up in the center of a very prickly gorse bush. "How clever you are," hissed the cat.

"If only I'd shaved myself," lamented poor Timothy. "It'll be the first thing I do when I get home."

But he wasn't home yet, and he and the cat spent the next few hours dodging, and hiding, and dodging again. In the end they reached old Madge Moloney's cottage.

Madge hadn't gone to bed, because she had heard from one of her Lochrie-men friends that the magic milk had not reached the rath, and then she had seen Timothy's horse and cart go clattering past empty, and had guessed that the milkman was in trouble on the bog. So she had left her door open, with the light streaming out to guide Timothy.

How glad he and the cat were to get inside! In the lamp-light their whiskers were not nearly so bright, and when Madge had shut her door they both began to feel safe again. Timothy told her all that had happened to him, and Madge nodded her head up and down and up and down.

"Tell me now," she said. "Did you drink that milk?" And when Timothy agreed that both he and the cat had drunk milk that morning, Madge confessed the whole story of the little black cow, and how she had slipped the can into his cart while he wasn't looking.

"The milk had rath grass and herbs in it," she said. "And sure it nearly made Lochrie-men of the two of you."

She looked so sorry for the trouble that she had brought on him that Timothy could not help forgiving her. "Well, Madge, I'd have delivered the milk for you if only you'd told me about it," he said kindly. "Lucky there's no real harm done. If you let me stay till it's daylight I'll go home and shave off this beard, and that will be the end of the whole business."

But it wasn't, because the hair on Timothy's face is be-witched to this very day. He has to shave morning and night, and never dares to miss doing it. People in Bally-munty often joke with him about his clean-shaven face, but nobody but Madge knows the reason for it. The good-natured milkman doesn't hold it against her. He delivers the magic milk for her daily at the rath, and usually leaves her a little can of his own good milk to use in her tea.

"You've made a changed man of me," he says with a laugh.

As for the cat—her whiskers still shine at night, but she is careful to stay indoors at the fire after dark. She hasn't spoken to Timothy since. He sometimes wonders if she can't—or if she just doesn't bother. But there is a look in her two green eyes sometimes, when she is watching him shaving, and—well, it makes Timothy very glad that she *doesn't* say what's in her mind!

8

The House That Sean Built

WHEN SEAN O'LEARY DECIDED TO BUILD HIS NEW HOUSE IN the little valley that people called the Gentle Glen he was simply asking for trouble. But he would not be warned.

"It's the prettiest spot in the country," he said. "And if I can get old Red Hugh Kelly to agree to my marriage with his daughter Kate—well, I'll be needing a fine house for my bride. If the Gentle People don't want any neighbors, they can go and live somewhere else."

Well, of course, that was a very rude way to talk about the fairy people of the glen. They might not have minded Sean's house if he had asked them nicely for permission to build, but as it was they were feeling very sore and touchy about the whole matter.

The foundations had been dug and the work was getting

well under way when one of the workmen called Sean's attention to an odd little circle of toadstools that was growing in what was going to be the kitchen.

"They weren't there yesterday," he said. "It's a warning that's what it is."

"Rubbish!" said Sean angrily, kicking the toadstools away. "These things can spring up overnight. Warning indeed! I don't need to be warned about anything!"

The workman said nothing, but the next day the circle of toadstools had grown again, just as perfect a little ring of grayish white knobs as before. And at this all the builders laid down their tools and refused to work.

"The Gentle People will be getting annoyed with *us*!" they said. "This is dangerous work, and you're not paying us enough to cover the risk."

Sean was furious, but he was determined that his house was going up, toadstools or no toadstools, and he finally got the men to agree to finish the job—for much higher wages.

Up went the house, a fine two-storied building, which Sean hoped would impress Red Hugh Kelly. Kate herself was ready and willing to marry Sean, but Red Hugh had not yet given his consent.

"My girl won't marry unless she goes to a home that's fit for her," he had declared.

As soon as the house was finished, and he had moved into it himself, Sean invited Red Hugh to come over on a certain evening and see the place. Red Hugh accepted, and Sean spent a busy day polishing the windows, and washing the floors, and leaving everything neat.

It was when he was washing the kitchen floor that he saw a neat little circle of toadstools, apparently growing through the floorboards!

At first he thought he was imagining things, and then he seized a shovel and brush, swept the nasty things away and threw them on the rubbish heap. Then he gathered a bunch of fresh flowers and brought them into the kitchen—and there was a little circle of toadstools, just as before.

A cold shiver went down Sean's spine. He dropped the flowers and seized the brush and shovel again. But this time the toadstools refused to brush away. The brush skidded over them, and there they stayed. When Sean dug at them with the shovel they merely gave off a horrible, damp, musty smell and stayed firmly where they were.

This was awful! Red Hugh would soon arrive, and he would certainly think toadstools were an odd decoration for the kitchen floor. In desperation, Sean pulled the table over the circle, and draped it with his best plush tablecloth. And not a moment too soon, for there was Red Hugh at the door, wearing his best blue suit in honor of the visit, and with his red hair and beard neatly combed by Kate.

"Welcome, and see the fine home I've built for the best girl in Ireland," cried Sean.

"Looks all right, so far," admitted Red Hugh. "But smells funny. Must be damp. I won't let Katy come to a damp house."

"It's the smell of the new plaster," said Sean. "Come, and I'll show you round."

Well, Red Hugh was pleased, although he was too cautious to say so outright. But when they had gone round the house, and Sean begged him to sit down at the kitchen table to discuss the wedding, over a glass of good porter, Red Hugh did not refuse.

"Here's to my darling Kate," proposed Sean, lifting his glass. But just as he was drinking he felt something under the table pushing against his knees, and he slopped his porter down his shirt front and went pale. Red Hugh felt something pushing against his knees, too, but he thought it must be a dog making friendly advances, and he put down a hand.

"Good doggy," he said, and patted. Somehow the thing under the table wasn't nice to pat. It felt cold and smooth and unfriendly, and Red Hugh pushed back a little from the table.

"It's—it's a new sort of support for the table," said Sean weakly, although he knew only too well that it was nothing of the kind. It was the circle of toadstools which had grown rapidly.

"Doesn't leave much room for one's legs," snorted Red Hugh, and raised his glass. And just at that minute the table rose about a foot into the air and jogged his elbow.

"That's a nasty trick," shouted Red Hugh, as the porter spilled down his beard and coat. "I don't hold with modern gadgets. Tables that shoot up and down and so on! You'd better put ordinary, old-fashioned furniture in, Sean my lad, or Kate won't put a foot inside your new house."

"Certainly," said poor Sean, and at that the table slowly tipped up, so that the jug of porter and Sean's glass slid down the slope and landed on Red Hugh's knees.

Well, that finished it. With his best blue suit ruined, Red Hugh threw the table aside and gazed in horror at the great toadstools.

"So that's what you were hiding," he shouted. "Toadstools! Nasty, unhealthy fungus, and probably poisonous, too. I'm not letting my daughter come here to be poisoned. Toadstools in the kitchen, indeed!" And he stamped off in a dreadful rage, leaving Sean simply brokenhearted.

Now most people, in Sean's place, would have left the house, and gone as far away from the Gentle Glen as they could go. But Sean was too upset to think of what the toadstools might still do to him. He just wanted to crawl off up the stairs to his bed, pull the clothes over his head, and feel thoroughly miserable. And that is what he did, but he wasn't left very long undisturbed.

You see, the position of Sean's bed happened to be exactly above the place in the kitchen where the toadstools had been steadily growing and about an hour after Sean had gone upstairs he suddenly noticed that the bed was beginning to rock to and fro. He was almost too scared to sit up and look, but at last he did so, and then he howled and dived under the clothes again. The giant toadstools had broken through the floor boards and were pushing up into the room.

"I'll never get out of this alive," cried Sean. "I wish I'd never set foot in the Glen. Indeed I do!"

Wishing didn't help matters. The bed rose until it was pressing against the ceiling, and what would have happened, had not the outer walls of the house collapsed with the swelling of the toadstools, nobody will ever know. Anyway, Sean, still trembling under the bedclothes, felt the bed sailing through the air, and downwards, with the house crashing around it.

"I'll be killed!" he wailed. But he wasn't, because the Gentle People didn't want to kill him, merely to frighten him, and the next minute he was sitting up in bed, outside in the open air, looking at a ring of simply gigantic toadstools, as tall as trees, with little bits of the roof of his fine house still clinging to them.

"Don't you think it's really time you got up out of your bed," said a voice, and Sean saw a bent old man with a long beard standing by his bed. The moonlight shone on the old man's face, which was stern, but not really angry. "Sean, Sean!" he said. "Why did you force me to do this to you, you silly, stubborn fellow?"

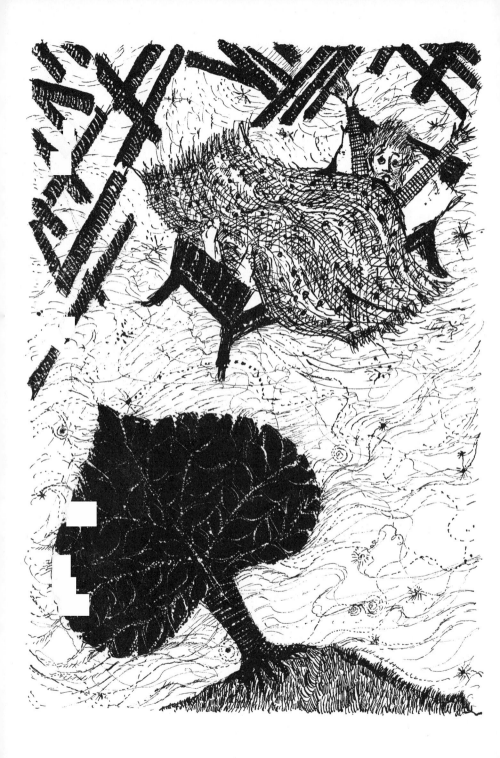

"Well, I've been properly punished," said poor Sean. "Not only is my house wrecked, but Kate will never be allowed to marry me now."

"And don't you deserve it," said the old man. "If you'd so much as asked leave to build here—instead of insulting the Gentle People, and ordering them to go elsewhere."

"I do deserve it," agreed Sean. "I'm really sorry," and he was going to dive under the bedclothes again when the old man caught the blankets and wrenched them away.

"Then get up, like a man, and face your problems," he cried. "How can I help you if you hide in bed. And help you I will—for my people don't hold grudges where they've been given a proper apology. I know you're sorry, Sean, and I'll get my people to build up your house for you again."

"Don't bother, sir. I don't need a house when I can't marry Kate," said Sean. "But thank you kindly all the same."

"We'll talk to Red Hugh," said the old man. "I'd like to see pretty Kate Kelly in the Gentle Glen. Leave that to me. Leave everything to me!"

Well, Sean left everything to the old man—indeed he could do nothing else, for a deep sleep fell upon him, and when he woke he was in bed in his house, and could have believed that the whole thing was a dream but for three things. The first was that the house was twenty yards further up the glen. The second was that there was a neat circle of toadstools in the grass of the front lawn. And the third was that the old man was standing beside the circle.

"Hurry up, Sean," he said. "Come along to Red Hugh's with me."

So off they went and were greeted by a furiously angry Red Hugh and a weeping Kate.

75

"I am Sean O'Leary's nearest neighbor in the Gentle Glen," said the old man. "And I've come with him to ask for the hand of your daughter Kate."

"Well, of all the cheek," bellowed Red Hugh. "After last night! After showing me those poisonous toadstools in the kitchen. The place isn't fit for a pig to live in!"

"There are no toadstools in Sean's kitchen," said the old man firmly. "There's a little ring of them in the grass before the house, that's all. You're telling stories, Red Hugh."

"And I have a fine story to tell," bellowed Red Hugh. "I saw them."

"And came home with his clothes soaking in porter, didn't he, Kate?" said the old man. "Dear, dear, dear. And then thinks all the queer things he saw were really there. Dear, dear me. It's very sad!"

Red Hugh was speechless with rage, but he dashed off to the Gentle Glen, and found everything as the old man had said. And now, how could he refuse to let Kate marry Sean, when people could say that he had built the finest house in the country for her? Anyway, he just couldn't understand things any more. He had seen toadstools—and patted toadstools—yet no toadstools were there. He hung his red head, and admitted that he was defeated.

Well, Kate was the prettiest bride that the people of the Gentle Glen had ever seen, and they always sent her the best of good fortune. Neither Sean nor Kate ever saw any of their Gentle neighbors, not even the old man. But the circle of toadstools is still growing before their house, and Kate weeds carefully around them, and keeps them well watered in dry weather.

9

Danny and the Fairy Dancers

DANNY DOLAN WAS THE VERY BEST DANCER IN Carrickmore, or for many miles around. Jigs, reels, or hornpipes—it was all the same to Danny, and people used to say there must be magic in his feet because they never became tired.

Well, when Danny had carried home all the medals and cups that could be won, the very proudest girl in Carrickmore was Brigid Anne O'Donnell. Now that was natural enough, for Brigid Anne was Danny's sweetheart, and nobody minded when she boasted about his dancing. But the people did mind the fact that Danny boasted so much about himself. In fact, there was not a more conceited young man in the length and breadth of Ireland.

"They've seen nothing yet," boasted Danny. "Wait

until the next *Feis* Week, and then I'll show them how to dance."

"But you've shown them already," said Brigid Anne. "Unless you're going to make some new steps and figures? Is that it?"

"Wait and see," said Danny mysteriously.

Now everybody in the district knew the stories that were told of the fairy dancing that took place at night at the crossroads two miles from the town across the bog. The tinkers and the bogmen told how they had heard magical music of pipes and fiddles, and been forced to dance and dance with a crowd of gray shadows until they simply dropped with weariness. Well, what Danny was planning was to creep along to the crossroads, and see if he could watch the dancing, and maybe pick up a few new figures to do himself. He said nothing to Brigid Anne, but the first fine moonlight night away with him across the bog.

He heard the fairy music long before he reached the crossroads, and his feet began to twitch and then to hop and tap in spite of himself, and before he knew what was happening he was dancing—dancing—dancing as he had never danced before. There were strange gray figures dancing, too, the Gentle Folk of the bog. And then Danny noticed that somebody's stray cow, a black cat, and a tall, stout old tramp had been bewitched, too, by the music.

The tramp certainly seemed to be enjoying himself quite a lot, although he was hopping about far too slowly and heavily and getting in everyone's way. Danny collided with him three or four times, and began to get very annoyed.

"Can't you be more careful?" he shouted angrily.

"I only wish you had my poor old feet to dance with," said the tramp piteously. "But you're young and proud, so you are."

Well, just at that very moment, a fairy horn sounded over the bog, to warn the Gentle Folk that it would soon be dawn, and at that the music went faster and faster in a final dance. Even Danny could hardly keep going, and then suddenly the music stopped, the gray figures glided away, and Danny flopped down at the roadside to get his breath. So did the cow, the cat, and the tramp who promptly fell asleep and began to snore loudly.

Proud Danny didn't like his company at all, and tired as he was he scrambled up and stumbled off homewards. How heavy and sore his feet were! Never had it been so hard to drag them along, and then, as it began to get light, he looked down at them and his heart stood still.

These cracked old boots did not belong to him. Where were his neat new shoes? And for that matter, where were his feet, for poor Danny began to become horribly certain that these aching things he was walking with were not his own at all! They looked much bigger than his feet, and they kept shuffling and limping, and when somebody's dog appeared and sniffed suspiciously, one of the feet made a kick at it without Danny's leg's permission—so that Danny nearly overbalanced and the dog began to bark wildly.

This was dreadful. Somehow the tramp's wish, just as the fairy horn blew, had bewitched him. Trembling, poor Danny hurried home, and the feet clattered against things and tripped over a mat in the kitchen, so that his father and mother, who were still in bed, called to him to be quiet. Danny was almost afraid to take off the old boots, and yet —he just *had* to see what sort of feet he had got. They were very dirty feet anyway! Danny was so disgusted that he got a basin of water and began to wash them, and then he saw that they had corns, and bunions, and long ragged nails.

"Oh, my goodness," wailed Danny. "They're awful!"

And the feet were so indignant that they kicked over the basin of water with a clatter.

"What *are* you doing, son," cried Danny's mother.

"Just going to bed," cried poor Danny, and he jumped into bed, wet feet and all, and pulled the clothes over his head.

Well, there he stayed, refusing to get up. In the first place the feet were much too big for his shoes, and in the second place Danny the proud wasn't going to go shuffling and hobbling through Carrickmore. He was still in bed when Brigid Anne called to the door to ask why he hadn't called for her to take her to the *ceilidhe*.

"Is Danny sick, Mrs. Dolan?" she asked, when she heard that her sweetheart was still in bed.

"Indeed I don't know what ails him," said Mrs. Dolan. "Come and talk to him, Brigid Anne, and maybe he'll tell you what is wrong."

So Brigid Anne went and stood by the bed. "Come to the dance, Danny," she begged.

"I'll never dance again," whispered Danny. "Don't tell anyone, Brigid Anne, but just look at these feet," and he stuck them out at the end of the bed.

Brigid Anne had to clap her hands across her mouth to smother a scream.

"I'll never be proud again," said Danny sadly, and he told her all that had happened to him. "Keep my secret, Brigid Anne, and then go away and find another sweetheart for yourself. Leave me here!" And Danny dived down under the bedclothes.

Well, Brigid Anne wasn't that kind of girl at all. She crept away, but not to look for another sweetheart. Instead, she set off for the crossroads to see if she could do anything about finding Danny's feet for him. The dance was in full

swing and, of course, she was soon drawn in amongst the fairy dancers and the various creatures that had been trapped by the magical music. Brigid Anne danced one set with a goat, and another with a collie dog, and then she noticed the big, stout old tramp, who was dancing with all the skill of Danny himself.

But the tramp wasn't happy at all. He was panting, and puffing, and his poor face was nearly purple. Brigid Anne was a kindhearted girl, and she danced over to him and slipped her hand under his arm.

"Lean on me, and rest a bit," she begged. "It's too much for you, at your age."

"Don't I know that, girl dear," panted the tramp. "But I had to come back here tonight to see if I could find the young fellow who went off with my feet. These are grand feet, entirely, and can dance every step that was ever invented, but they go too fast for my old body."

"You've got Danny's feet then," cried Brigid Anne. "And he won't get out of bed because he's got yours. Oh, please, can't we do something to change them back again?"

"We can do nothing tonight," puffed the old man, "for we'll be dancing here until daybreak. But get your Danny here tomorrow night. If we can be together, and wishing hard, when the fairy horn blows, maybe things will right themselves."

Well, it was morning when a very tired Brigid Anne crept home, but the next evening she went down to Dolans' and asked to see Danny.

"He must be in a fever," wailed Danny's mother. "He's kicking so much that he's torn his sheet to shreds, but he won't let me send for the doctor."

When Brigid Anne explained the plan to Danny he was only too ready to try it, but he simply couldn't get into his shoes. And Mrs. Dolan had found the tramp's old boots in the kitchen and indignantly thrown them away, wondering how such nasty things had come to be in *her* kitchen. But then Danny tried a pair of his father's good Sunday boots, and they fitted perfectly. So he and Brigid Anne slipped as quietly as possible out of the house, and made for the cross-roads, Danny hobbling along as best he could and trying to keep in the shadows.

The dance was in full swing again, and Danny and Brigid Anne were swept into it by the bewitching music. The tramp was already there, and Danny watched his own feet in amazement as they hopped and tapped. They had obviously learned some new steps since he had last had them under him!

"Get close to him," whispered Brigid Anne. "And keep wishing hard."

It was easy to say—"Get close to him." But that was just the one thing that Danny couldn't do because, try as he would, he could not catch up with the flying feet. He hopped about on the aching corns and bunions, but he simply could not get near to the tramp.

"Wait for me," he wailed.

"The feet won't let me," panted the tramp, who was only too willing to wait for his own feet, if he could have done so.

So the night wore on, and the hour when the fairy horn would blow drew nearer and nearer, and still Danny and the tramp could not get close to one another. Poor Brigid Anne, tired as she was by her second night of dancing, was simply at her wit's end. And when, at last, she saw the first faint gray streaks in the sky, she gave up hope and burst out crying.

And at that something happened! Danny stopped worrying about his feet and dashed to comfort Brigid Anne. And Danny's own feet, still with the tramp attached to them, forgot to dance and rushed to Brigid Anne, too. Crash, the two men collided, and down they fell together, kicking and struggling, and at the same moment the fairy horn blew, and the girl cried out: "Oh, I wish you were both yourselves again!"

Well, when the dancers had fled and Danny and the tramp had sorted themselves out, they found that they had got back their own feet.

"I'll never be rude to an old person again," cried Danny thankfully, trying out a few dance steps in his joy. "I deserved it all, proud and conceited as I was."

"I never thought," said the tramp slowly, "that I'd be glad to feel my corns aching. I should never have complained about them. They're *lovely* corns, so they are!"

Well, that's very nearly the end of the story. Danny danced at the next *Feis,* and won all the prizes. People said that he had never danced so well, and indeed his feet seemed to have kept some of the magic that had been in them. How proud Brigid Anne was of her sweetheart, but Danny was never too proud of himself now.

"It's not that I'm very clever," he used to say. "I'm just a lucky fellow, that's all. Luckier than I deserve."

But Danny's father could never understand why he couldn't find his best Sunday boots. He hunted high up and low down for them, and they just were not to be found. Of course, when the tramp got back his own feet, they happened to be wearing Mr. Dolan's boots, and while Danny's father was hunting for them the boots were miles and miles away. And the tramp found them so comfortable, and they suited his corns so well, that he felt as if he had indeed got a new pair of feet.

10

Vincie and the Magic Voices

THERE IS A CERTAIN TOWNLAND IN IRELAND WHERE THE people take it absolutely for granted that one can go and listen to the voices of the Magic Folk any time one wishes. All one has to do is to climb up the steep hill, called Old Hogan's Mountain, to the opening between two rocks that leads into a dark, unknown cave. There one can shout "Hullo" or "Good Day" to the Magic Folk, and can be sure that they will answer.

Old Hogan had grazed his sheep on his mountain since the days when he was not Old, but Young Hogan, and he was very proud of *his* Magic Voices. He did not mind in the least that the children of the district had made a path up to the cave. Many of them had to pass his mountain on their way to school, and they would race each other up to the top to shout their greetings to the Good People. The only child that Old Hogan did *not* like to see was Vincie.

Vincie was a very nasty boy! He didn't look bad—in fact he looked as if butter wouldn't melt in his mouth. He was clever at his school work, and Master O'Carroll could not find fault with him. But he suspected, and quite rightly, that Vincie was secretly at the bottom of every piece of mischief and disorder that took place in the school. The trouble was that Master O'Carroll couldn't catch him out.

Old Hogan had noticed for a long time that the Voices were sulky and indignant after every visit from Vincie. So on a certain nice evening, when he saw Vincie climbing the mountain on his way home from school, he followed.

When Vincie got to the cave he waited for a minute to get his breath, and then he started to shout all the insulting things he could think of.

"Bah! I'm not afraid of you! Stupid things! Bah-ah! Boo-oo! Bah-ah-ah!"

And the Voices shouted back his insults as fast as they could.

"You ought to be ashamed of yourself," cried Old Hogan, who had reached the cave by this time. "A big lad like you!"

"Bah!" cried Vincie again. He shook a stone loose from the wall that Old Hogan had built up to keep his sheep from wandering into the cave. "Here you are, Voices," cried Vincie and hurled the stone down into the cave mouth, where it clattered down, and down and down into the darkness. "I'm not afraid. Bah-ah-ah."

"You—you—you!" spluttered Old Hogan. "You sound just like a sheep—indeed you do, you rude boy. I'm telling you, you'll be sorry for this."

"You'll be sorry for this!" echoed the Voices furiously.

But Vincie merely shouted, "Bah-ah-ah-ah!" again, and raced off down the mountain and home to his tea.

His mother was a widow, and she had been out at work and had not got the kettle to the boil when her son dashed in and flung his schoolbag down.

"Vincie, will you go to the stack for a few dry turfs for me?" she asked nervously. "I'm sorry it's not ready."

"Bah-ah!" shouted Vincie angrily.

"Oh, Vincie," cried the widow.

Vincie had not meant to say "Bah." It had said itself, and when he opened his mouth to tell his mother that he hadn't meant it—well "Bah-ah-ah," came out again, but this time softly and apologetically. He was so frightened that he grabbed up the turf basket and dashed out to the stack, where he tried again to speak.

But nothing would come from Vincie's mouth but the Bah of a sheep. He tried and tried, until his mother came to see what was keeping him. He wasn't able to tell her, so he said nothing at all for the rest of the evening. The widow thought he was sulking which, unfortunately, he very often did, so she left him alone until the next morning.

Old Hogan was awakened very early the next day by a voice outside his window.

"Silly old fool Hogan!" said the voice.

Old Hogan got out of bed and went to the window, but nobody was to be seen, only a sheep, who stood with her eyes and mouth wide open.

"You old idiot you!" said the sheep, and turned big, appealing eyes up to her master.

Old Hogan shook his head sadly and went back to bed. He was dreaming, and he might as well do it in comfort in his cozy bed, he told himself, and pulled the clothes up over his ears.

Outside, the unfortunate sheep would have cried if she had only known how to go about it. It was bad enough to have found that she couldn't Bah, and to have got a human voice that made the other sheep run away from her! But to have got a nasty, bold voice that insulted her dear master!

She looked up into the bright morning sky and thought what a black day it was for her.

It was black for Vincie, too. He had hoped that the sheep's voice would have worn off by morning, but it was just as bad as ever. He *couldn't* go to school like that. When his mother picked up his schoolbag and cap after breakfast he shook his head violently and backed away from her.

"Now, Vincie," she said. "You've kept up this silliness long enough. Indeed, I don't know what your poor father would have said if he could have seen what a difficult boy you've turned into lately. You have my poor heart broken."

Vincie's face burned with shame, but he still shook his head and put a hand to his throat.

"Have you lost your voice?" demanded the widow. "I don't wonder after all the loud yelling you were doing last night—pretending to be a sheep! Well, I'm taking you down to Dr. Ryan, and if he says so then into the school you go, and no nonsense about it!"

Vincie was quite eager to have his throat examined, and went with his mother down to the doctor's house in the town. But Dr. Ryan shook his head.

"I can't see anything the matter with him," he said, peering down Vincie's throat. "I'd say he's playing on you, ma'am. Take no notice and he'll soon speak."

"Bah-ah-ah-ah!" cried Vincie suddenly, right into the doctor's face. "Bah-ah-ah!"

"See what I mean," cried Dr. Ryan, springing back in

alarm. "Definitely a case of Boldness Fever, ma'am!"

The widow was furious! "How could you be so rude to the doctor?" she cried, and she marched Vincie down to the schoolhouse and watched until he had gone in.

He was late by this time, but he went to his seat without apologizing to Master O'Carroll, because he knew only too well what would happen to him if he opened his mouth.

The Master noticed this rudeness, and called Vincie up at once to say his lesson from the day before. But Vincie stood—the clever boy who always knew his work—and not a word could he say.

"Sit down and learn it," snapped Master O'Carroll, and from that minute he kept watching Vincie. He had been longing for years to catch Vincie out in doing wrong, because he knew who was responsible for the disorder that was in the school. But Vincie had always been too clever for him. Today, however, Master O'Carroll felt quite hopeful, and his right hand began to itch with a longing to give Vincie the beating he deserved. Three times he called the boy up to answer questions, but Vincie would shake his head, and put a hand to his throat, as if it hurt. So Master O'Carroll could only wait and watch.

It seemed to Vincie that he was getting through the morning quite well, with his pretended sore throat. But just as a little of his usual cheekiness was coming back to him, something awful happened.

"Master O'Carroll is the biggest fool in this town!" said a voice suddenly, and it was undoubtedly Vincie's voice.

"What did you say?" asked the Master quietly and very politely.

"Old Blather!" said the voice. "Think yourself clever, don't you?"

It *was* Vincie's voice, and as the boy was *in* the school it never occurred to the Master that the voice could possibly be outside. But it was, because the unfortunate sheep had come looking for her own voice, and she was just under the window beside Vincie's desk.

Master O'Carroll waited no longer. He came striding down the room to Vincie, who was so terrified that he tried to speak.

"Bah-ah-ah-ah!" he yelled into the Master's face. "Bah!"

Well—the Master didn't succeed in beating Vincie as much as he would have liked, because the boy twisted away and ran off bleating loudly, but he did succeed in making a fairly good job of it all the same. He quite enjoyed himself.

Now, to go back to Old Hogan. From the moment when he got up that morning properly, the old fellow had been chuckling at what he thought was his dream.

"So I thought my own sheep was talking to me. That was a good one," he chuckled.

But a little later he stopped chuckling, for he heard a great bleating, mixed with a sneering boy's voice, and there were Vincie and the sheep coming along down the path from the town.

You see, Vincie didn't know where to go. He couldn't go back to school, and he couldn't go home, so it seemed the easiest thing to keep with the sheep, even though the sheep was abusing him loudly all the way.

The sheep was enjoying herself. She had found that Vincie's voice had a simply endless supply of nasty things to say, and it amused her that the voice was saying them to its owner.

It didn't amuse Vincie. He had never realized quite how rude he had always been, or quite how it hurt to be called names, and he felt his face getting redder with real shame.

And he had never really been ashamed in his life before.

Well, when Old Hogan heard the abuse and the Bah-ing he seized his stick and hurried along the path to meet the two. "Can't you even leave the poor innocent animal in peace, you young rascal?" he shouted, waving the stick above his head.

"Bah-ah-ah!" wailed poor Vincie, actually dropping on his knees before Old Hogan.

"Impudent lump," said the sheep, and went up and rubbed her black face against Old Hogan's trousers. "Old miser. Silly old man Hogan."

"Bah-ah-ah," protested Vincie, pointing to his mouth.

Well, anybody else but Old Hogan would have been completely dumbfounded, or would have thought himself dreaming or ill and gone to a doctor or back to bed. But Old Hogan had lived for many years near the cave of the Magic Voices, so he could take something like this more or less in his stride, as the saying goes. He pulled out his pipe, lit it, and looked from Vincie to the sheep and the sheep to Vincie and back again to the sheep.

"So that's the way of it," he said, letting out a puff of smoke. "The boy deserves it, beyond a doubt, but it's a bit hard on my sheep. Come up with you both to the cave and I'll see if I can get the Magic Folk to put things right."

They gladly scrambled up behind him to the cave mouth.

"Now listen," said Old Hogan very softly into the cave. "If you'll give the lad back his voice, Good People, I think I can promise that he will use it properly in the future. I think he's learned his lesson."

"Oh yes, indeed," cried Vincie in his own voice. "Oh, dear Mr. Hogan, thank you, thank you. Indeed, I'll never forget this."

And the sheep gave a loud happy Bah-ah and dashed off.

Vincie never did forget the lesson he had learned. He apologized to Master O'Carroll, to his mother, and to Dr. Ryan, and from that day he was the politest boy in the whole district. And whenever he passed Old Hogan's mountain he never forgot to call out a greeting to the old man or to climb up to the cave to speak to the Voices.

And the Magic People have completely forgiven Vincie, for whenever he calls, "Hullo. Good day and good luck to you. Hullo," back come the softest, sweetest voices in the world, and return the greeting to him. And they keep echoing soft, friendly murmurs as he trudges off down the hillside.

The Author

Kathleen Green is a native of Ireland. She began writing poetry at the age of seven and a few years later she had two volumes of her verse privately published. When she was sixteen, her stories and poetry began to appear in magazines and by the age of nineteen Miss Green had begun to have her fairy stories broadcast by the BBC radio station. To date she has published approximately three hundred stories in newspapers and magazines.

At the age of twenty-four Miss Green gave up her position as editor of the features page of a provincial newspaper to join the Radio Eireann Symphony Orchestra as violist and she is still with the Symphony. Although a professional musician, she has continued to write.

The stories in this volume have a special meaning for their author, for as she says, "The conception of this book . . . came during one of the blackest periods of my life. I had just lost my father and inherited a delicate mother and an over-draft at the bank. My health was so bad that I was in danger of losing my job in the Orchestra . . . It was a case of going under, or rising above the waves, and my sense of humor saved me—hence this book."